To Frank and Helen Daley, my parents,
who made every Christmas unforgettable.

—DDM

To Cindy.
It is very appropriate to dedicate to you this story of faith, and of giving.
Much love.

—RC

ZONDERKIDZ

The Legends of Christmas Treasury
This is a compilation of previously published stories:

The Legend of St. Nicholas (ISBN 978-0-310-73115-3)
Copyright © 2007 by Dandi Daley Mackall
Illustrations © 2014 by Richard Cowdrey

The Legend of the Candy Cane (ISBN 978-0-310-73012-5)
Copyright © 1997 by Lori Walburg
Illustrations © 2012 by Richard Cowdrey

The Legend of the Christmas Cookie (978-0-310-74767-3)
Copyright © 2008 by Dandi Daley Mackall
Illustrations © 2015 by Richard Cowdrey

Requests for information should be addressed to:
Zonderkidz, 3900 *Sparks Drive SE, Grand Rapids, Michigan* 49546

This edition: ISBN 978-0-310-75743-6 (hardcover)

Editor: Barbara Herndon
Art direction and design: Kris Nelson/StoryLook Design

Printed in China

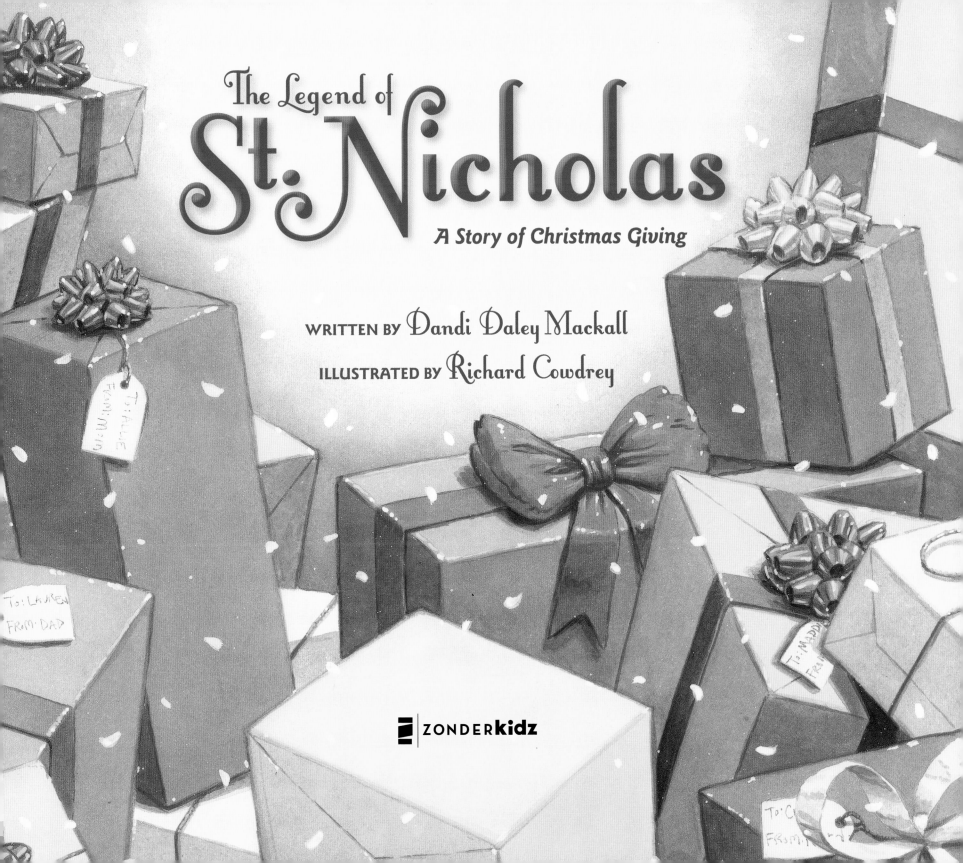

The Legend of St. Nicholas

A Story of Christmas Giving

WRITTEN BY Dandi Daley Mackall

ILLUSTRATED BY Richard Cowdrey

ZONDERkidz

N ick followed his dad through the snow-dusted parking lot. "Not my idea of fun," he muttered.

"Hey, you're the one who waited until the last minute to buy Christmas gifts for your little brothers," Dad reminded him.

"True," Nick admitted. Why was it so much easier to think about getting gifts than giving them?

Nick spotted a skinny Santa ringing a bell and collecting for the poor. Dad handed Nick some money for Santa's kettle. Nick thought about adding something from his own wallet, but he was hoping to have enough left to get himself something.

Once inside the crowded store, Nick smelled hot dogs and popcorn. Scratchy Christmas music played overhead.

"You get your gifts, and I'll see to this list your mother gave me," Dad called, disappearing into the sea of shoppers.

Nick headed for the toy aisle, but a baseball glove caught his eye. A few minutes later, he heard a deep voice saying his name.

Christmas
Bobby - Game
Nick - BB Glove
Kris - Doll
Rich - Paints
Cindy - Books

The voice belonged to a store Santa. "Santa used to go by the name 'Nick,' or 'Saint Nicholas,'" he heard the Santa say to a group of children in the "Elf Room." Nick remembered waiting for his parents in that room when he was a little kid. "A long, long time ago," the store Santa continued, "in a country far across the sea, a boy named Nicholas was born."

Nick leaned against the doorway and listened.

Nicholas's parents were very rich. They traveled all over the world with their son. When Nicholas was eight, they visited beautiful gardens in the Far East. Nicholas noticed children begging for food.

When Nicholas turned ten, his parents took him to the West. Nicholas couldn't sleep at night because he kept thinking about the longing eyes of the children in the streets, children who had certainly never owned a toy.

On his twelfth birthday, Nicholas and his family journeyed to the North. Nicholas waved to the children playing in the snow. "Why aren't they wearing coats and hats?" he asked.

His parents exchanged sad looks. "They probably don't own coats and hats, Nicholas," his father said.

A few years later, they visited the Holy Land, where baby Jesus had been born that first Christmas. "In this holy place, God gave us the greatest gift ever given," Nicholas's father remarked. "Imagine how much God loves us to give us his only son."

"To honor and celebrate God's amazing gift, three wise kings brought gifts for the Christ child," Nicholas's mother said, as the church bells rang out.

Not long after they returned home, Nicholas's parents died. Nicholas felt lost and alone. He had plenty of money, but no idea what to do with his life. He looked to his friends for help.

"If I had that much money," said Joseph, "I'd pay all of our bills because my father is out of work."

"I would buy my mother a warm coat," Thomas added.

Phoebe gazed at the stars. "My two sisters want to marry, but we don't have the money that's required from the bride's family. If I had the money, I would give it to my sisters for this dowry." She sighed. "And if I had enough, I would do the same for myself."

Nicholas knew that his friends would never get their wishes ... unless ...

That night, Nicholas talked things over with God.
"Father, could this be the work you have for me?"

As if in answer, the church bells rang. Nicholas
remembered what his mother had said about the wise
kings bringing gifts to baby Jesus. He thought of what
his father said about Jesus being the greatest gift.
What better time to give gifts than on Jesus' birthday!

Nicholas could barely hold in his excitement. First, he tromped through falling snow to Joseph's house. He opened a window and tossed in enough gold coins to allow them to buy their own home.

Next, he woke the town tailor and bought his finest coat. Nicholas ran all the way to Thomas's house and stuffed the coat through the open shutters.

Nicholas's last stop was Phoebe's house. He tied coins into three bags for three dowries and searched for an open window. Nicholas was about to give up when he looked to heaven and prayed for God's guidance. That's when he thought of the chimney.

On Christmas Day, Nicholas's friends came running to his house.

"It's a miracle!" Joseph exclaimed. "God must have heard my prayers."

"We were given a gift as well," Thomas began. "My mother hasn't taken off her new coat since she found it this morning."

Phoebe's eyes sparkled like sunlight on snow. "My sisters will marry next month." She smiled at Joseph. "Now I, too, can marry. We don't know who else to thank, so we thank God."

Overcome with joy, Nicholas understood his mission in life. This is how he would celebrate Christmas from now on.

When the story ended, Nick shook himself. A part of him was back with Nicholas. He could imagine how good it must have felt to secretly give his friends what they had wanted most. Nick had almost forgotten why people gave presents at Christmas. He wanted to feel that same joy of giving.

"Nick! Time to go!" Dad walked up, his arms full of shopping bags.

"We can't go yet, Dad!"

Nick never imagined buying gifts could be so much fun. He found just the right toys for his brothers. Then he spent everything he had left on toys for the poor. "I wish I had enough to fill the whole collection box!" he told Dad.

Nick felt sure he'd never look at Christmas the same way. He wanted to remember the gifts of Saint Nicholas, the gifts of the wise kings, and most of all, God's gift of baby Jesus.

Nick never imagined buying gifts could be so much fun. He found just the right toys for his brothers. Then he spent everything he had left on toys for the poor. "I wish I had enough to fill the whole collection box!" he told Dad.

Nick felt sure he'd never look at Christmas the same way. He wanted to remember the gifts of Saint Nicholas, the gifts of the wise kings, and most of all, God's gift of baby Jesus.

Traditions of Christmas Giving

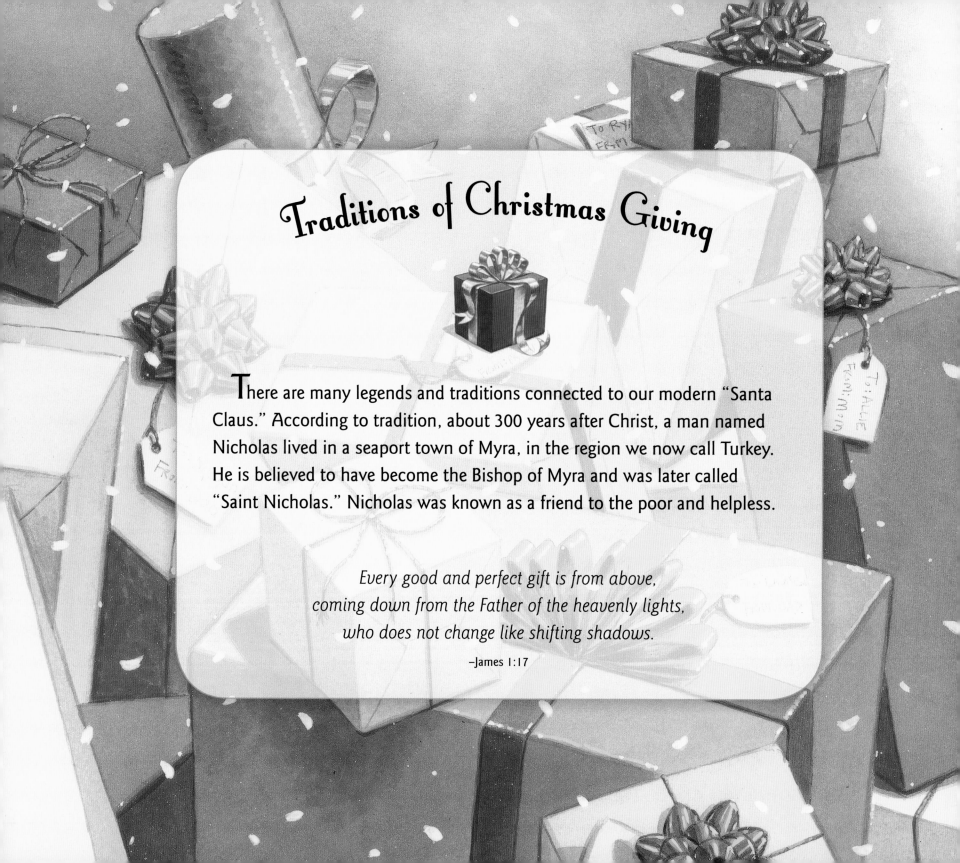

There are many legends and traditions connected to our modern "Santa Claus." According to tradition, about 300 years after Christ, a man named Nicholas lived in a seaport town of Myra, in the region we now call Turkey. He is believed to have become the Bishop of Myra and was later called "Saint Nicholas." Nicholas was known as a friend to the poor and helpless.

Every good and perfect gift is from above,
coming down from the Father of the heavenly lights,
who does not change like shifting shadows.

–James 1:17

To Jack and Lois Walburg,
My parents, mentors, and best friends.
—LW

To Maddie, Joel, Eliot, Hayla, & Daisy,
May the story of the candy cane and the truth of Christ's love live in your hearts.
—RC

The Legend of the Candy Cane

The Inspirational Story of Our Favorite Christmas Candy

WRITTEN BY Lori Walburg

ILLUSTRATED BY Richard Cowdrey

One dreary evening in the depths of November a stranger rode into town. He stopped his horse in front of a lonely storefront. The windows were boarded shut and the door was locked fast. But the man looked at it, smiled, and said, "It will do."

All through the short, gray days and the long, dark nights of November, the man worked.

The townspeople could hear the faint *pam pam pam* of his hammer and the *snish snish snish* of his saw.

They could smell the sweet, clean scent of new lumber and the deep, oily smell of new paint.

But no one knew who the man was or what he was doing.

The mayor hoped the man was a doctor, to heal his illness. The young wives hoped he was a tailor, to make beautiful dresses. The farmers hoped he was a trader, to exchange their grain for goods.

But the children had the strongest, deepest wish of all. A wish they did not tell their parents. A deep, quiet, secret wish that none of them said out loud.

No one spoke to the man. No one asked if he needed help. They just waited. And watched. And wondered. And wished.

But one small girl
watched and wondered,
waited and wished longer
than she could stand.
And one snowy day she
knocked at the stranger's
door. "Hello," she said.
"My name is Lucy. Do you
need some help?"

The man smiled warmly
and nodded. Then he
opened the door, and Lucy
stepped inside.

A long counter ran down
the side of the room. Bare
shelves filled the opposite
walls. In the back were
dozens and dozens of
barrels and crates.

"Could you help me
unpack?" the man asked.

Lucy's heart sank at the sight of all the boxes. What if they were only barrels of nails and bags of flour?

But she removed her dripping boots and hung her coat on a peg. On stocking feet, she crossed the rough wooden floor and knelt beside a crate.

"Please. Open it," the man urged.

Slowly, Lucy put her hand into the box and pulled out an object wrapped in tissue. Round and heavy, it almost slipped through her fingers. Lucy trembled a little as she unwrapped it.

It was a glass jar.

Lucy gave the man a puzzled look. "Go on," his nod said.

So she unpacked another glass jar, and another, and another, until she was completely surrounded by jars of all shapes and sizes. Tall and thin. Round and squat. Jars with lids and jars without.

"Now," the man said, "for something to put inside." And he pulled over a huge crate stamped with a strange word.

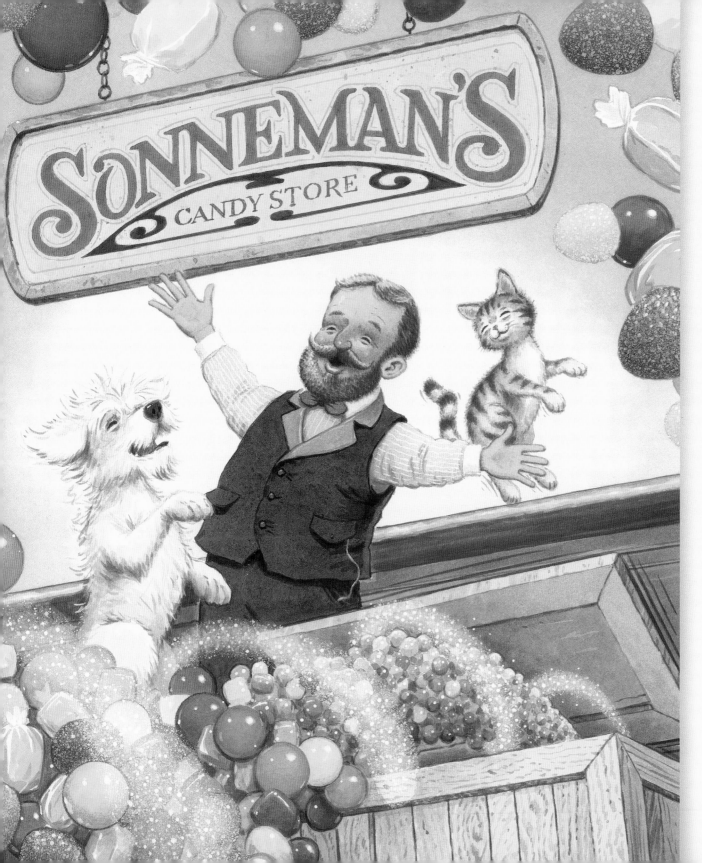

As Lucy unpacked, her eyes lit up.

It was candy. Her favorite candy. Gumdrops!

"Try some," the man said.

She popped one in her mouth. Now she could hardly unwrap fast enough. Peppermint sticks! Taffy! Lollipops! Chewing gum!

Wide-eyed, she looked at the man.

"We wished—," Lucy said.

"Yes, I know," said the man. "And here it is. Welcome to Sonneman's Candy Store. I am John Sonneman."

Soon the small store was filled with candies, gleaming in their glass jars. Raspberry suckers and tiny lemon drops. Brightly colored jawbreakers and long tangles of licorice. Pink and white peppermints for church and butterscotch balls for company.

Then, in the very last package in the very last crate, was a candy Lucy had never seen before, a red-and-white striped candy stick with a crook on the end.

"What is this?" Lucy asked.

"This," Mr. Sonneman explained, "is a candy cane. It is a very special Christmas candy."

"Why?" Lucy asked.

"Tell me," Mr. Sonneman said, "what letter does it look like?"

Lucy took the candy and turned it in her hand.

"J!" she said.

"Yes." Mr. Sonneman smiled. "J for Jesus, who was born on Christmas day."

"Now, turn it over. What does it remind you of?"

Lucy turned the candy in her hand. She peered down intently. "I know!" she said finally. "It's like a shepherd's staff."

"Who were the first to find out about Jesus' birth?" Mr. Sonneman asked.

"Shepherds in the field," Lucy answered, "watching over their flocks by night."

"But Mr. Sonneman, what are the stripes for?" Lucy asked.

The man's eyes grew sad. "The prophet Isaiah said, 'By his stripes we are healed.' Before he died on the cross, Jesus was whipped. He bled terribly. The red reminds us of his suffering and his blood."

"But then," Mr. Sonneman continued, "the candy is white as well. When we give our lives to Jesus, his blood washes away our sins, making us white and pure as snow."

"That," he said, "is the story of the candy cane."

"Is it a secret?" Lucy asked.

Mr. Sonneman looked at her for a long moment. "It's a story that needs to be told," he said. "Will you help me share it?"

It was now the depths of December. The town was whipped round by blizzard winds. For days, the sun hid itself.

But every morning, Mr. Sonneman and Lucy ventured out. They wore heavy woolen coats and bright handknit scarves. And in their stiff, mittened fingers, they each held a bag.

They went to every house in town. They traveled to every farm in the country. They knocked on every door. In every home, they told the story, they left a small gift, and they gave an invitation.

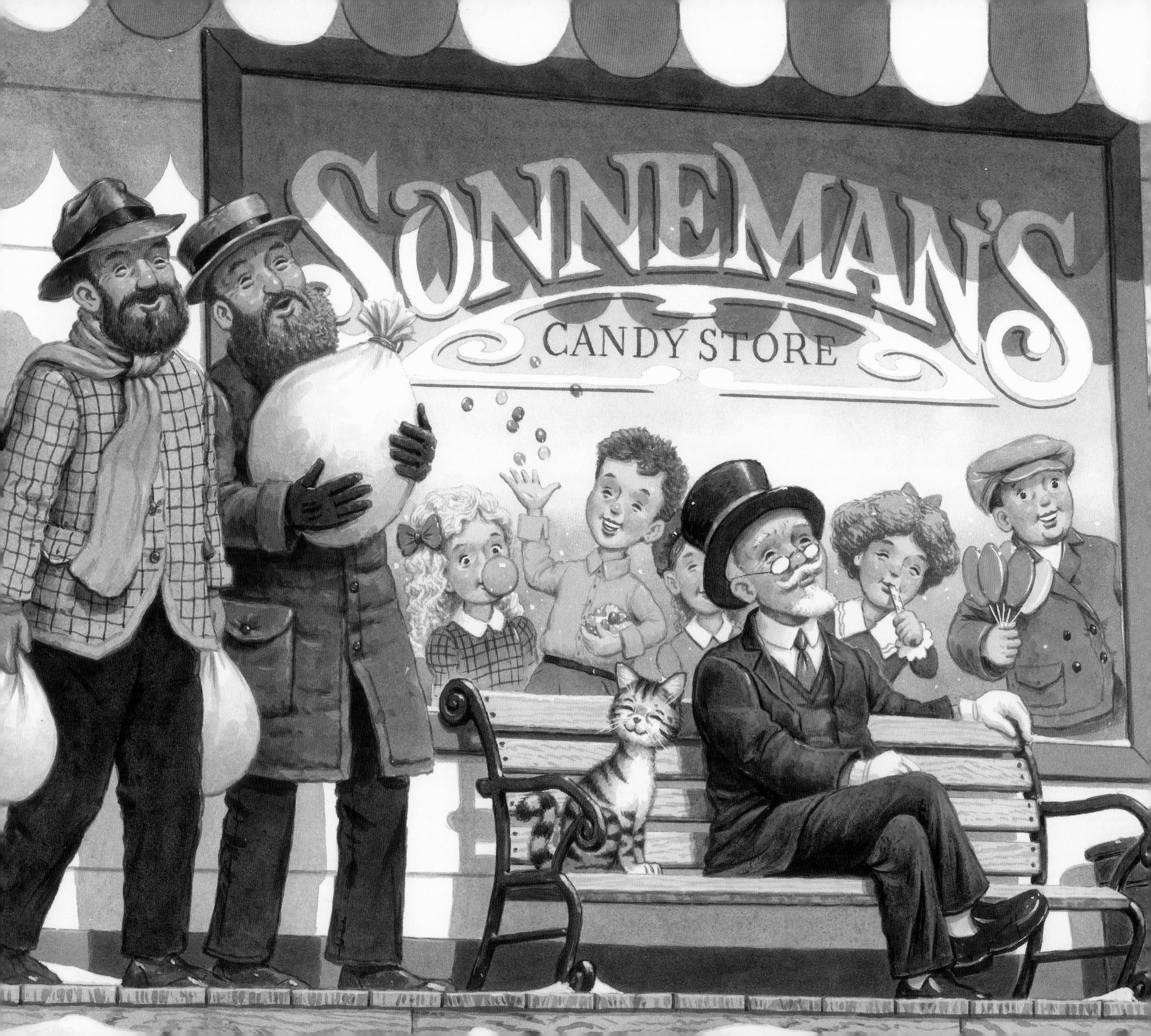
SONNEMAN'S
CANDY STORE

On the afternoon of Christmas Eve, the sun finally broke through the clouds.

And Sonneman's Candy Store officially opened.

The mayor came, feeling better than he'd felt in days. The young wives came, dressed in beautiful smiles. The farmers came, eager to trade grain for Christmas gifts. The children ran in dizzy circles.

Yes, their wish had come true.

Yes, they had come to share in the opening of the candy store.

But they shared something more. Something bigger. Something better.

On that Christmas Eve, they shared the story of the candy cane.

They told the miracle of Christ's birth.

The misery of his death.

And the mercy of his love.

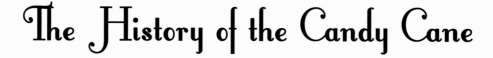

The History of the Candy Cane

The traditional candy cane was born over 350 years ago when mothers used white sugar sticks as pacifiers for their babies. Around 1670, the choirmaster of Cologne Cathedral in Cologne, Germany, bent the sticks into canes to represent a shepherd's staff. He then used these white candy canes to keep the attention of small children during the long Nativity service.

The use of candy canes during the Christmas service spread throughout Europe. In northern Europe, sugar canes decorated with sugar roses were used to brighten the home at Christmas time.

In the mid 1800s, the candy cane arrived in the United States when a German-Swedish immigrant in Wooster, Ohio, decorated his spruce tree with paper ornaments and white sugar canes.

The red stripe was added to the candy cane at the turn of the century, when peppermint and wintergreen were added and became the traditional flavors for the candy cane. Some sources say that a candy maker in Indiana developed the candy cane as a witness of Christ's love. While we may never know the full history of the candy cane, we can share in the truth behind its symbol, the truth of Christ's birth and redemption, and the gift of his love.

To Katy Mackall, April Coffman,
Melissa and Michelle Kinney,
who love those cookies!

—DDM

To Rebekah Marie.......welcome!

—RC

The Legend of the Christmas Cookie

Sharing the True Meaning of Christmas

WRITTEN BY Dandi Daley Mackall   ILLUSTRATED BY Richard Cowdrey

ZONDERkidz

In the distance Jack heard the lonely cry of a train whistle. He leaned into the icy wind and crossed the railroad tracks toward home.

Home. Their house hadn't felt like a home since Jack's dad had hopped a freight train West to find work. Now, on Christmas Eve, word came that Dad couldn't make it home for Christmas.

As Jack stepped inside, the heavenly scent of sweet bread and licorice wafted from the kitchen. *Cookies!*

But it couldn't be. Mom put every penny Dad sent home straight into the cookie jar. There hadn't been a single cookie in that jar for over a year.

"Jack?" Mom called. She was in the kitchen, stirring something in a giant bowl.

"You're really making cookies?" Jack still couldn't believe it.

His mother smiled weakly. "They're for the needy at church."

Jack tried to hide his disappointment. He'd been feeling pretty needy himself lately.

"Unpack the cookie boards, Jack," said his mother, not missing a *beat*, *beat*, *beat* on the dough.

Jack unwrapped the carved wooden shapes— shepherd, star, camel, king, man and woman kneeling, baby, and cross. The last mold was an angel the size of his hand.

"It's so big!" Jack exclaimed. He could make a cookie like that last a whole week.

Jack's mother helped him roll the dough into a smooth oval. It was hard work.

"Why are we going to so much trouble to make Christmas cookies people are just going to eat anyway?" Jack asked.

His mom picked up the big angel mold and dusted it with flour. "Maybe it's time you heard why people first started making Christmas cookies."

Jack watched as his mother pressed the angel board into the dough. "The story goes back hundreds of years," she began, "back to the Middle Ages. In the Old Country—where your father's people lived—times were hard."

Jack rolled another batch of dough and wondered if times in the Middle Ages had been harder than they were right now, and if boys missed their fathers like he missed his.

The villagers couldn't afford school, so most couldn't read. As Christmas drew near, one family longed to help their neighbors discover the true meaning of Christmas.

"Let's carve figures to tell the story of Christ's birth!" the father, a woodcarver, suggested.

"But the villagers are hungry," his wife pointed out. "We should bake for them."

So the family worked together. The woodcarver whittled, scooping out wood until it formed the shape of an angel. He finished all the figures.

Then his wife mixed sweet dough to fill the molds.

When the cookies were done, the children decorated them with berries and colored sugar.

On Christmas Eve the woodcarver's family carried the cookies to the village. Soon a crowd gathered. As his daughter held up the angel cookie, the woodcarver began: "Long ago an angel like this one brought us the most wonderful news: 'Today in the town of David a Savior has been born to you; he is Christ the Lord.'"

They recounted the whole story of Jesus' life as they handed out cookies to the amazed listeners.
Ever since that night, generations have passed down the art of making Christmas cookies and of

At the Christmas Eve service Jack thought of the woodcarver's family when the pastor read the same passage from Luke, the angel's announcement to the shepherds.

As Jack stood to sing "Hark! The Herald Angels Sing," his gaze fell on the stained-glass window. All of the figures were there—the star, the shepherd, Mary, Joseph, and baby Jesus. And above them was the angel. The window told the whole story, just like the Christmas cookies.

That night Jack dreamed of giant Christmas cookies. When he awoke, his mother was waiting. "Merry Christmas, Jack." She handed him the big angel cookie.

"For me?" Jack hugged his mother. But before he could take a bite, there was a knock at the door.

Jack froze. His mother raced past him to answer the door. It would be just like Dad to surprise them and show up on Christmas morning.

An old man stood in the doorway. "Could you spare a stranger a bite to eat?" he asked.

Disappointment choked off Jack's words and made his eyes water.

Jack could tell his mother was as let down as he was, but she invited the man to come in from the cold. "You're welcome to share our breakfast," she said.

The stranger ate fast without saying much. When he'd finished every last crumb, he thanked them and left.

Jack watched the man walk off toward the tracks. Jack hoped—prayed— that strangers had invited his dad to share their breakfast. Jack wished he'd taken the time to talk to the stranger, to wish him a Merry Christmas.

"Jack, don't forget your cookie," Mom said.

Jack ran his finger along the grooves of the angel's wings. He could almost hear the old woodcarver. "That's it!" he exclaimed.

Jack tore out of the house and ran to catch up with the stranger.

"What's this?" asked the stranger, taking the cookie Jack offered him.

"It's yours," Jack explained. "And there's a story that goes with it." Then right there, beside the railroad tracks, under a gray sky that promised snow, Jack began: "Long ago an angel like this one brought us the most wonderful news: 'Today in the town of David a Savior has been born to you; he is Christ the Lord.'"

The Original Christmas Cookie

In the Schwaben region of Southern Germany, Austria, and Switzerland, cookie boards called springerle molds were carved by craftsmen into shapes. In the Middle Ages the shapes were mainly religious. These cookies are still made today either by pressing dough into a mold or by rolling out the dough and imprinting it with specially designed rolling pins.